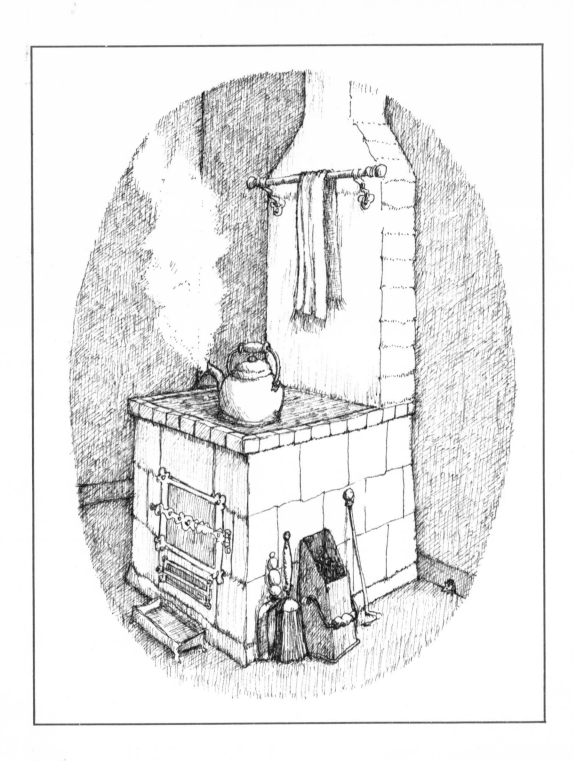

On the Little Hearth

*Words and music
for the popular Yiddish classic,
Oif'n Pripitchik*

by Gabriel Lisowski

Holt, Rinehart and Winston / New York

Acknowledgments:
Words and music by Mark Warshawski (1848-1907)
This lullaby, created and sung during
a time of threat and great unrest for the Jews
of eastern Europe, is still popular today.

Thanks are due to Professor Shalom Altman,
director of the Tyson Music Department,
Gratz College, Philadelphia, for his help
and guidance.

English translation by Miriam Chaikin

10   9   8   7   6   5   4   3   2   1

Library of Congress Cataloging in Publication Data

Lisowski, Gabriel.
   On the little hearth   Oif'n pripitchik.

   English and Yiddish.
   SUMMARY: An illustrated version with music
of a popular Jewish lullaby created and sung during
a time of great threat and unrest for the Jews
of eastern Europe.
   [1. Lullabies] I. Warshawski, Mark, 1848–1907.
Oyfn pripetshok. English & Yiddish. 1978.
II. Title.   III. Title: Oif'n pripitchik.
PZ8.3.L6360n   821   78-4270   ISBN 0-03-039931-9

On the little hearth
a lively fire burns
casting warming rays,

as the *rebbe* teaches
all the little ones
to say the *A-lef, Beys.*

"Little dears," he pleads,
"strive to memorize
the letters of God's law,
say them one more time
and still another time,
Ko-metz A-lef, Aw.

Now, my dearest ones,
you can't understand,
but you will one day know,

the strength and beauty of
the words they form

the comfort of their glow.

Though it's hard at first,
remember, darling ones,
what you are striving for,
study leads us to
a grasp of Torah
—who has need of more?

And if, God forbid,
this land casts us out
we will find new hope,
golden words we've learned
will be a source of strength
and teach us how to cope."

So remember, dears,
strive to memorize
the letters of God's law,
say them one more time
and still another time,
Kometz A-lef, Aw.

Zogtje noch amol

Un take noch amol

Kometz A-lef Aw.

ON THE LITTLE HEARTH   OIF'N PRIPITCHIK   אויפֿן פּריפּעטשיק

On the little hearth	Oif'n pripitchik	אױפֿן פּריפּעטשיק ברענט אַ פֿײַערל,

On the little hearth
a lively fire burns
casting warming rays,
as the *rebbe* teaches
all the little ones
to say the *A-lef, Beys.*

Oif'n pripitchik
Brent a fai-eril
Un in shtub iz heys.
Un der rebbe lerent
Kleyne kinderlach
Dem . . A-lef, Beys.

אױפֿן פּריפּעטשיק ברענט אַ פֿײַערל,
און אין שטוב איז הײם.
און דער רבי לערנט קלײנע קינדערלעך
דעם אלף־בית.

Refrain:

"Little dears," he pleads,
"strive to memorize
the letters of God's law,
say them one more time
and still another time,
Ko-metz A-lef, Aw.

Refrain:

Zetje kinderlach
Gedenktje tai-ere
Vos ir lerent daw
Zogtje noch amol
Un take noch amol
Kometz A-lef Aw.

רעפֿריין:

זעט זשע, קינדערלעך, געדענקט זשע, טײַערע,
װאָס איר לערנט דאָ,
זאָגט זשע נאָך אַ מאָל און טאַקע נאָך אַ מאָל:
קמץ־אלף: אַ!

2.

Now, my dearest ones,
you can't understand,
but you will one day know
the strength and beauty of
the words they form
the comfort of their glow.

2.

Az ir vet, kinder, elter vern,
Vet ir aleyn farshteyn,
Vifl in di oysyes lign trern,
Un vi fil geveyn.

2.

אַז איר װעט, קינדער, עלטער װערן,
װעט איר אַלײן פֿאַרשטײן,
װיפֿל אין די אותיות ליגן טרערן,
און װי פֿיל געװײן.

Refrain

3.

Though it's hard at first,
remember, darling ones,
what you are striving for,
study leads us to
a grasp of Torah
—who has need of more?

Refrain

3.

Lerent kinder
Hot nit moyre,
Yeder onhoyb iz shver,
Gliklech der vos hot
Gerlerent toyre
Tsi darf der mentsh nach mer.

3.

לערענט, קינדער, האָט ניט מורא,
יעדער אָנהויב איז שװער;
גליקליך דער װאָס האָט געלערענט תּורה,
צי דאַרף דער מענש נאָך מער?

Refrain

4.

And if, God forbid,
this land casts us out
we will find new hope,
golden words we've learned
will be a source of strength
and teach us how to cope."

Refrain

4.

Az ir vet kinder
Dem goles shlepn,
Oysgemutshet zain
Zolt ir fun di oysyes
Koyech shepn
Kukt in zey arain.

4.

אַז איר װעט, קינדער, דעם גלות שלעפּן,
אויסגעמוטשעט זײַן,
זאָלט איר פֿון די אותיות כּוֹח שעפּן,
קוקט אין זיי אַרײַן!

So remember, dears,
strive to memorize
the letters of God's law,
say them one more time
and still another time,
Kometz A-lef, Aw.

Zetje kinderlach
Gedenktje tai-ere
Vos ir lerent daw
Zogtje noch amol
Un take noch amol
Kometz A-lef Aw.

זעט זשע, קינדערלעך, געדענקט זשע, טײַערע,
װאָס איר לערנט דאָ,
זאָגט זשע נאָך אַ מאָל און טאַקע נאָך אַ מאָל:
קמץ־אלף: אַ!

Zogtje noch amol
Un take noch amol
Kometz A-lef Aw.

Zogtje noch amol
Un take noch amol
Kometz A-lef Aw.

Oi - f'n pri - pit - chik brent a fai - e - ril Un in shtub iz heys.
On the lit - tle hearth, A live - ly fi - re burns Cast - ing warm - ing rays.

1.

Un der reb - be le - rent kley - ne kin - der - lach dem__ A - lef Beys.
As the reb - be teach - es all the lit - tle ones to say the A - lef Beys.

2.

dem __ A - lef Beys. Zet - je kin - der - lach Ge - denkt - je tai - e - re
say the A - lef Beys. "Lit - tle dears," he pleads, "strive to mem - o - rize the

Vos ir le - rent daw. Zogt - je noch a - mol un ta - ke noch a - mol
let - ters of God's law. Say them one more time and still an - oth - er time

1.

2.

Ko - metz A - lef Aw.   Ko - metz A - lef Aw.
Ko - metz A - lef Aw."   Ko - metz A - lef Aw."

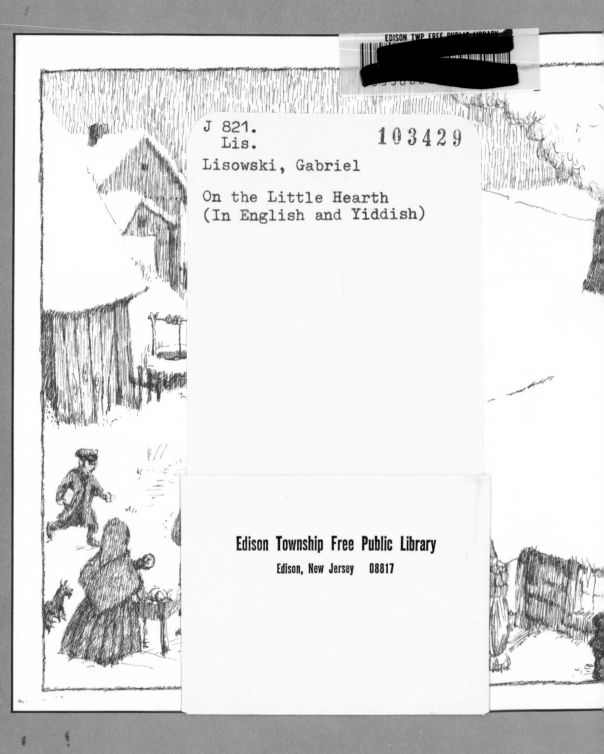